The wizards really needed someone to help them catch the wicked witch, but **who?**

5

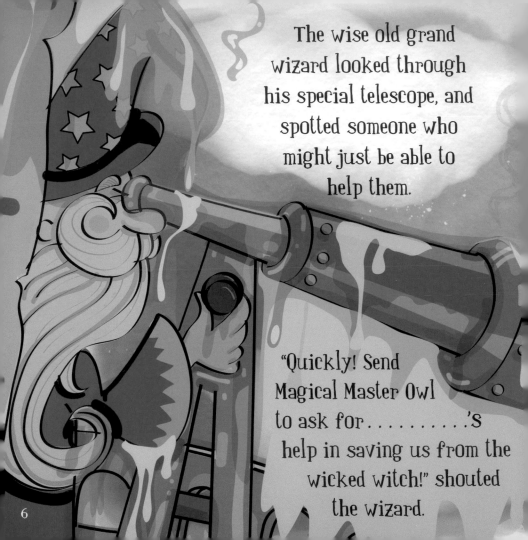

The wise old grand wizard looked through his special telescope, and spotted someone who might just be able to help them.

"Quickly! Send Magical Master Owl to ask for . . . .'s help in saving us from the wicked witch!" shouted the wizard.

6

TO: . . . .
A magical story
for a magical you

From:

Oh no!
The wizards
were in
BIG trouble!

A wicked witch had cast
an evil spell completely covering
their magical kingdom in
slimy and extremely smelly goo!
ALL of the wizards were trapped!

4

Magical Master Owl knew he had
to help so he flapped and fluttered
as swiftly as he could to find the boy
spotted through the telescope.

7

"WHIZZ BAM!"
.... said, as he waved
his pretend wand towards
his dog Ruffles.

"Oh Ruffles you are
supposed to turn into a
flying dog."

.... SO wanted
to be a Wizard.

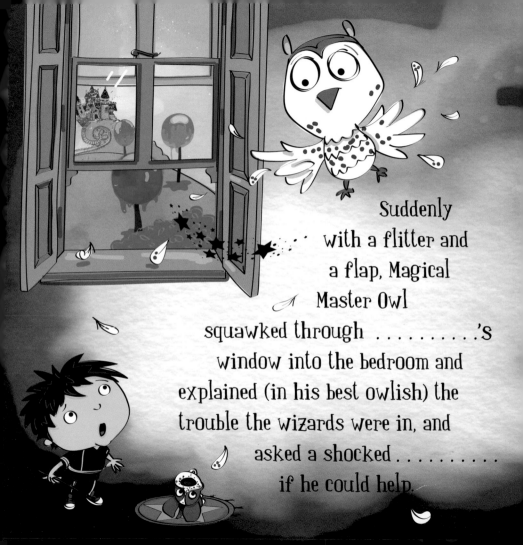

Suddenly
with a flitter and
a flap, Magical
Master Owl
squawked through . . . .'s
window into the bedroom and
explained (in his best owlish) the
trouble the wizards were in, and
asked a shocked . . . .
if he could help.

"Of course!"
said a delighted . . . .

So Magical Master Owl squawked
three times, flapped his wings
four times, and with a WHIZZ
PUFF, a broomstick, cape and
magic wand suddenly appeared!

. . . . put on the cape,
picked up the wand,
and jumped on his brand
new broomstick.

Quick as a flash
they zoomed out of
. . . . 's window to look
for the wicked witch.

11

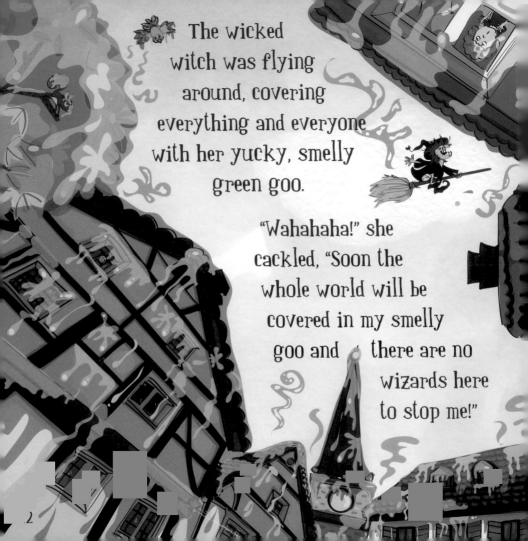

The wicked witch was flying around, covering everything and everyone with her yucky, smelly green goo.

"Wahahaha!" she cackled, "Soon the whole world will be covered in my smelly goo and there are no wizards here to stop me!"

2

But little did she
realise that . . . .
was on his way.

He zoomed
under bridges...

...and over houses,
looking for the
goo-spreading
witch.

13

Suddenly Ruffles made
a big booming **bark**.
His super-smelling nose had caught
a whiff of the wicked witch, but she
was too far away for . . . .
to cast a spell on her.

. . . . clicked
his heels, gripped his
broomstick even tighter,
and zoomed at supersonic speed
towards the wicked witch.

15

Finally . . . .
caught up with
the wicked witch.

"Who are you?" the wicked
witch sneered, as she
launched a **massive** dollop
of **sticky** green
goo at . . . .

16

With lightning speed
. . . . waved his magic wand.
"BIZZ POP GOO I will stop you!" he shouted.
A huge brightly-coloured umbrella appeared.
deflecting all of the smelly goo.

17

The wicked witch squealed
with anger, zapping another
dollop of smelly green goo
towards . . . .

"WHIZZ SPLAT
send me your hat!"
. . . . shouted.

The witch's hat flew off
her head, catching all of her
smelly green goo. Yuck!

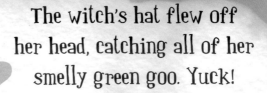

The witch couldn't
believe what this boy
wizard was doing!

18

"ZIP ZAP, you will be trapped in your hat!"
. . . . .cast another spell.

The witch's goo-filled hat flew back to her, squashing down over her head, squishing her in the smelly green goo.

Hurray the **wicked witch** was trapped!

19

A triumphant . . . . took the wicked witch back to the wizards' castle.

All the slippery, slimy green goo had now gone thanks to . . . . breaking the bad witch's horrible spell.

The wizards were so grateful to
. . . . that they let him keep the cape,
broomstick AND magic wand!

. . . . finally felt like a true wizard!

The End